The Repairman

I0548899

The Repairman

Harry Harrison

ÆGYPAN PRESS

This novel first appeared in the February, 1958, issue of *Galaxy*.

Harry Harrison was also known by the name Henry Maxwell Dempsey.

Special thanks to Greg Weeks, Susan Carr, and the Online Distributed Proofreading Team (which can be found at http://www.pgdp.net).

The Repairman
A publication of
ÆGYPAN PRESS

www.aegypan.com

Being an interstellar trouble shooter wouldn't be so bad . . . if I could shoot the trouble!

The Old Man had that look of intense glee on his face that meant someone was in for a very rough time. Since we were alone, it took no great feat of intelligence to figure it would be me. I talked first, bold attack being the best defense and so forth.

"I quit. Don't bother telling me what dirty job you have cooked up, because I have already quit and you do not want to reveal company secrets to me."

The grin was even wider now and he actually chortled as he thumbed a button on his console. A thick legal document slid out of the delivery slot onto his desk.

"This is your contract," he said. "It tells how and when you will work. A steel-and-vanadium-bound contract that you couldn't crack with a molecular disruptor."

I leaned out quickly, grabbed it and threw it into the air with a single motion. Before it could fall, I had my Solar out and, with a wide-angle shot, burned the contract to ashes.

The Old Man pressed the button again and another contract slid out on his desk. If possible, the smile was still wider now.

"I should have said a *duplicate* of your contract — like this one here." He made a quick note on his secretary plate. "I have deducted 13 credits from your salary for the cost of the duplicate — as well as a 100-credit fine for firing a Solar inside a building."

I slumped, defeated, waiting for the blow to land. The Old Man fondled my contract.

"According to this document, you can't quit. Ever. Therefore I have a little job I know you'll enjoy. Repair job. The Centauri beacon has shut down. It's a Mark III beacon. . . ."

"*What* kind of beacon?" I asked him. I have repaired hyperspace beacons from one arm of the Galaxy to the other and was sure I had worked on every type or model made. But I had never heard of this kind.

"Mark III," the Old Man repeated, practically chortling. "I never heard of it either until Records dug up the specs. They found them buried in the back of their oldest warehouse. This was the earliest type of beacon ever built — by Earth, no less. Considering its location on one of the Proxima Centauri planets, it might very well be the first beacon."

I looked at the blueprints he handed me and felt my eyes glaze with horror. "It's a monstrosity! It looks more like a distillery than a beacon — must be at least a few hundred meters high. I'm a repairman, not an archeologist. This pile of junk is over 2000 years old. Just forget about it and build a new one."

The Old Man leaned over his desk, breathing into my face. "It would take a year to install a new beacon

— besides being too expensive — and this relic is on one of the main routes. We have ships making fifteen-light-year detours now."

He leaned back, wiped his hands on his handkerchief and gave me Lecture Forty-four on Company Duty and My Troubles.

"This department is officially called Maintenance and Repair, when it really should be called trouble-shooting. Hyperspace beacons are made to last forever — or damn close to it. When one of them breaks down, it is *never* an accident, and repairing the thing is never a matter of just plugging in a new part."

He was telling *me* — the guy who did the job while he sat back on his fat paycheck in an air-conditioned office.

He rambled on. "How I wish that were all it took! I would have a fleet of parts ships and junior mechanics to install them. But its not like that at all. I have a fleet of expensive ships that are equipped to do almost anything — manned by a bunch of irresponsibles like *you.*"

I nodded moodily at his pointing finger.

"How I wish I could fire you all! Combination space-jockeys, mechanics, engineers, soldiers, con-men and anything else it takes to do the repairs. I have to browbeat, bribe, blackmail and bulldoze you thugs into doing a simple job. If you think you're fed up, just think how I feel. But the ships must go through! The beacons must operate!"

I recognized this deathless line as the curtain speech and crawled to my feet. He threw the Mark III file at me and went back to scratching in his papers. Just as I reached the door, he looked up and impaled me on his finger again.

"And don't get any fancy ideas about jumping your contract. We can attach that bank account of yours on Algol II long before you could draw the money out."

I smiled, a little weakly, I'm afraid, as if I had never meant to keep that account a secret. His spies were getting more efficient every day. Walking down the hall, I tried to figure a way to transfer the money without his catching on — and knew at the same time he was figuring a way to outfigure me.

It was all very depressing, so I stopped for a drink, then went on to the spaceport.

*B*y the time the ship was serviced, I had a course charted. The nearest beacon to the broken-down Proxima Centauri Beacon was on one of the planets of Beta Circinus and I headed there first, a short trip of only about nine days in hyperspace.

To understand the importance of the beacons, you have to understand hyperspace. Not that many people do, but it is easy enough to understand that in this *non*-space the regular rules don't apply. Speed and measurements are a matter of relationship, not constant facts like the fixed universe.

The first ships to enter hyperspace had no place to go — and no way to even tell if they had moved. The beacons solved that problem and opened the entire universe. They are built on planets and generate tremendous amounts of power. This power is turned into radiation that is punched through into hyperspace. Every beacon has a code signal as part of its radiation and represents a measurable point in hyperspace. Triangulation and quadrature of the beacons works for navigation — only it follows its own rules. The rules are complex and variable, but they are still rules that a navigator can follow.

For a hyperspace jump, you need at least four beacons for an accurate fix. For long jumps, navigators use as many as seven or eight. So every beacon is important and every one has to keep operating. That is where I and the other trouble-shooters came in.

We travel in well-stocked ships that carry a little bit of everything; only one man to a ship because that is all it takes to operate the overly efficient repair machinery. Due to the very nature of our job, we spend most of our time just rocketing through normal space. After all, when a beacon breaks down, how do you find it?

Not through hyperspace. All you can do is approach as close as you can by using other beacons, then finish the trip in normal space. This can take months, and often does.

This job didn't turn out to be quite that bad. I zeroed on the Beta Circinus beacon and ran a complicated eight-point problem through the navigator, using every beacon I could get an accurate fix on. The computer gave me a course with an estimated point-of-arrival as well as a built-in safety factor I never could eliminate from the machine.

I would much rather take a chance of breaking through near some star than spend time just barreling through normal space, but apparently Tech knows this, too. They had a safety factor built into the computer so you couldn't end up inside a star no matter how hard you tried. I'm sure there was no humaneness in this decision. They just didn't want to lose the ship.

*I*t was a twenty-hour jump, ship's time, and I came through in the middle of nowhere. The robot analyzer chuckled to itself and scanned all the stars, comparing them to the spectra of Proxima Centauri. It finally rang a bell and blinked a light. I peeped through the eyepiece.

A fast reading with the photocell gave me the apparent magnitude and a comparison with its absolute magnitude showed its distance. Not as bad as I had thought — a six-week run, give or take a few days. After feeding a course tape into the robot pilot, I strapped into the acceleration tank and went to sleep.

The time went fast. I rebuilt my camera for about the twentieth time and just about finished a correspondence course in nucleonics. Most repairmen take these courses. Besides their always coming in handy, the company grades your pay by the number of specialties you can handle. All this, with some oil painting and free-fall workouts in the gym, passed the time. I was asleep when the alarm went off that announced planetary distance.

Planet two, where the beacon was situated according to the old charts, was a mushy-looking, wet kind of globe. I tried to make sense out of the ancient directions and finally located the right area. Staying outside the atmosphere, I sent a flying eye down to look things over. In this business, you learn early when and where to risk your own skin. The eye would be good enough for the preliminary survey.

The old boys had enough brains to choose a traceable site for the beacon, equidistant on a line between two of the most prominent mountain peaks. I located the peaks easily enough and started the eye out from the first peak and kept it on a course directly toward the second. There was a nose and tail radar in the eye and I fed their signals into a scope as an amplitude curve. When the two peaks coincided, I spun the eye controls and dived the thing down.

I cut out the radar and cut in the nose orthicon and sat back to watch the beacon appear on the screen.

The image blinked, focused — and a great damn pyramid swam into view. I cursed and wheeled the eye in circles, scanning the surrounding country. It was flat, marshy bottom land without a bump. The only thing in a ten-mile circle was this pyramid — and that definitely wasn't my beacon.

Or wasn't it?

I dived the eye lower. The pyramid was a crude-looking thing of undressed stone, without carvings or decorations. There was a shimmer of light from the top and I took a closer look at it. On the peak of the pyramid was a hollow basin filled with water. When I saw that, something clicked in my mind.

*L*ocking the eye in a circular course, I dug through the Mark III plans — and there it was. The beacon had a precipitating field and a basin on top of it for water; this was used to cool the reactor that powered the monstrosity. If the water was still there, the beacon was still there — inside the pyramid. The natives, who, of course, weren't even mentioned by the idiots who constructed the thing, had built a nice heavy, thick stone pyramid around the beacon.

I took another look at the screen and realized that I had locked the eye into a circular orbit about twenty feet above the pyramid. The summit of the stone pile was now covered with lizards of some type, apparently the local life-form. They had what looked like throwing sticks and arbalasts and were trying to shoot down the eye, a cloud of arrows and rocks flying in every direction.

I pulled the eye straight up and away and threw in the control circuit that would return it automatically to the ship.

Then I went to the galley for a long, strong drink. My beacon was not only locked inside a mountain of handmade stone, but I had managed to irritate the things who had built the pyramid. A great beginning for a job and one clearly designed to drive a stronger man than me to the bottle.

Normally, a repairman stays away from native cultures. They are poison. Anthropologists may not mind being dissected for their science, but a repairman wants to make no sacrifices of any kind for his job. For this reason, most beacons are built on uninhabited planets. If a beacon *has* to go on a planet with a culture, it is usually built in some inaccessible place.

Why this beacon had been built within reach of the local claws, I had yet to find out. But that would come in time. The first thing to do was make contact. To make contact, you have to know the local language.

And, for *that*, I had long before worked out a system that was fool-proof.

I had a pryeye of my own construction. It looked like a piece of rock about a foot long. Once on the ground, it would never be noticed, though it was a little disconcerting to see it float by. I located a lizard town about a thousand kilometers from the pyramid and dropped the eye. It swished down and landed at night in the bank of the local mud wallow. This was a favorite spot that drew a good crowd during the day. In the morning, when the first wallowers arrived, I flipped on the recorder.

After about five of the local days, I had a sea of native conversation in the memory bank of the machine translator and had tagged a few expressions. This is fairly easy to do when you have a machine memory to work with. One of the lizards gargled at another one and the second one turned around. I tagged this expression with the phrase, "Hey, George!" and waited my chance to use it. Later the same day, I caught one of them alone and shouted "Hey, George!" at him. It gurgled out through the speaker in the local tongue and he turned around.

When you get enough reference phrases like this in the memory bank, the MT brain takes over and starts filling in the missing pieces. As soon as the MT could give a running translation of any conversation it heard, I figured it was time to make a contact.

I found him easily enough. He was the Centaurian version of a goat-boy — he herded a particularly loathsome form of local life in the swamps outside the town. I had one of the working eyes dig a cave in an outcropping of rock and wait for him.

When he passed next day, I whispered into the mike: "Welcome, O Goat-boy Grandson! This is your grandfather's spirit speaking from paradise." This fitted in with what I could make out of the local religion.

Goat-boy stopped as if he'd been shot. Before he could move, I pushed a switch and a handful of the local currency, wampum-type shells, rolled out of the cave and landed at his feet.

"Here is some money from paradise, because you have been a good boy." Not really from paradise — I had lifted it from the treasury the night before. "Come back tomorrow and we will talk some more," I called after the fleeing figure. I was pleased to notice that he took the cash before taking off.

After that, Grandpa in paradise had many heart-to-heart talks with Grandson, who found the heavenly loot more than he could resist. Grandpa had been out of touch with things since his death and Goat-boy happily filled him in.

I learned all I needed to know of the history, past and recent, and it wasn't nice.

In addition to the pyramid being around the beacon, there was a nice little religious war going on around the pyramid.

It all began with the land bridge. Apparently the local lizards had been living in the swamps when the beacon was built, but the builders didn't think much of them. They were a low type and confined to a distant continent. The idea that the race would develop and might reach *this* continent never occurred to the beacon mechanics. Which is, of course, what happened.

A little geological turnover, a swampy land bridge formed in the right spot, and the lizards began to wander up beacon valley. And found religion. A shiny metal temple out of which poured a constant stream of magic water — the reactor-cooling water pumped down from the atmosphere condenser on the roof. The radioactivity in the water didn't hurt the natives. It caused mutations that bred true.

A city was built around the temple and, through the centuries, the pyramid was put up around the beacon. A special branch of the priesthood served the temple. All went well until one of the priests violated the temple and destroyed the holy waters. There had been revolt, strife, murder and destruction since then. But still the holy waters would not flow. Now armed mobs fought around the temple each day and a new band of priests guarded the sacred fount.

And I had to walk into the middle of that mess and repair the thing.

It would have been easy enough if we were allowed a little mayhem. I could have had a lizard fry, fixed the beacon and taken off. Only "native life-forms" were quite well protected. There were spy cells on my ship, all of which I hadn't found, that would cheerfully rat on me when I got back.

Diplomacy was called for. I sighed and dragged out the plastiflesh equipment.

*W*orking from 3D snaps of Grandson, I modeled a passable reptile head over my own features. It was a little short in the jaw, me not having one of their toothy mandibles, but that was all right. I didn't have to look *exactly* like them, just something close, to soothe the native mind. It's logical. If I were an ignorant aborigine of Earth and I ran into a Spican, who looks like a two-foot gob of dried shellac, I would immediately leave the scene. However, if the Spican was wearing a suit of plastiflesh that looked remotely humanoid, I would at least stay and talk to him. This was what I was aiming to do with the Centaurians.

When the head was done, I peeled it off and attached it to an attractive suit of green plastic, complete with tail. I was really glad they had tails. The lizards didn't wear clothes and I wanted to take along a lot of electronic equipment. I built the tail over a metal frame that anchored around my waist. Then I filled the frame with all the equipment I would need and began to wire the suit.

When it was done, I tried it on in front of a full-length mirror. It was horrible but effective. The tail dragged me down in the rear and gave me a duck-waddle, but that only helped the resemblance.

That night I took the ship down into the hills nearest the pyramid, an out-of-the-way dry spot where the amphibious natives would never go. A little before dawn, the eye hooked onto my shoulders and we sailed straight up. We hovered above the temple at about 2,000 meters, until it was light, then dropped straight down.

It must have been a grand sight. The eye was camouflaged to look like a flying lizard, sort of a cardboard pterodactyl, and the slowly flapping wings obviously had nothing to do with our flight. But it was impressive enough for the natives. The first one that spotted me screamed and dropped over on his back. The others came running. They milled and mobbed and piled on top of one another, and by that time I had landed in the plaza fronting the temple. The priesthood arrived.

I folded my arms in a regal stance. "Greetings, O noble servers of the Great God," I said. Of course I didn't say it out loud, just whispered loud enough for the throat mike to catch. This was radioed back to the MT and the translation shot back to a speaker in my jaws.

The natives chomped and rattled and the translation rolled out almost instantly. I had the volume turned up and the whole square echoed.

Some of the more credulous natives prostrated themselves and others fled screaming. One doubtful type raised a spear, but no one else tried that after the pterodactyl-eye picked him up and dropped him in the swamp. The priests were a hard-headed lot and weren't buying any lizards in a poke; they just stood and muttered. I had to take the offensive again.

"Begone, O faithful steed," I said to the eye, and pressed the control in my palm at the same time.

It took off straight up a bit faster than I wanted; little pieces of wind-torn plastic rained down. While the crowd was ogling this ascent, I walked through the temple doors.

"I would talk with you, O noble priests," I said.

Before they could think up a good answer, I was inside.

*T*he temple was a small one built against the base of the pyramid. I hoped I wasn't breaking too many taboos by going in. I wasn't stopped, so it looked all right. The temple was a single room with a murky-looking pool at one end. Sloshing in the pool was an ancient reptile who clearly was one of the leaders. I waddled toward him and he gave me a cold and fishy eye, then growled something.

The MT whispered into my ear, "Just what in the name of the thirteenth sin are you and what are you doing here?"

I drew up my scaly figure in a noble gesture and pointed toward the ceiling. "I come from your ancestors to help you. I am here to restore the Holy Waters."

This raised a buzz of conversation behind me, but got no rise out of the chief. He sank slowly into the water until only his eyes were showing. I could almost hear the wheels turning behind that moss-covered forehead. Then he lunged up and pointed a dripping finger at me.

"You are a liar! You are no ancestor of ours! We will —"

"Stop!" I thundered before he got so far in that he couldn't back out. "I said your ancestors sent me as emissary — I am not one of your ancestors. Do not try to harm me or the wrath of those who have Passed On will turn against you."

When I said this, I turned to jab a claw at the other priests, using the motion to cover my flicking a coin grenade toward them. It blew a nice hole in the floor with a great show of noise and smoke.

The First Lizard knew I was talking sense then and immediately called a meeting of the shamans. It, of course, took place in the public bathtub and I had to join them there. We jawed and gurgled for about an hour and settled all the major points.

I found out that they were new priests; the previous ones had all been boiled for letting the Holy Waters cease. They found out I was there only to help them restore the flow of the waters. They bought this, tentatively, and we all heaved out of the tub and trickled muddy paths across the floor. There was a bolted and guarded door that led into the pyramid proper. While it was being opened, the First Lizard turned to me.

"Undoubtedly you know of the rule," he said. "Because the old priests did pry and peer, it was ruled henceforth that only the blind could enter the Holy of Holies." I'd swear he was smiling, if thirty teeth peeking out of what looked like a crack in an old suitcase can be called smiling.

He was also signaling to him an underpriest who carried a brazier of charcoal complete with red-hot irons. All I could do was stand and watch as he stirred up the coals, pulled out the ruddiest iron and turned toward me. He was just drawing a bead on my right eyeball when my brain got back in gear.

"Of course," I said, "blinding is only right. But in my case you will have to blind me before I *leave* the Holy of Holies, not now. I need my eyes to see and mend the Fount of Holy Waters. Once the waters flow again, I will laugh as I hurl myself on the burning iron."

*H*e took a good thirty seconds to think it over and had to agree with me. The local torturer sniffled a bit and threw a little more charcoal on the fire. The gate crashed open and I stalked through; then it banged to behind me and I was alone in the dark.

But not for long — there was a shuffling nearby and I took a chance and turned on my flash. Three priests were groping toward me, their eye-sockets red pits of burned flesh. They knew what I wanted and led the way without a word.

A crumbling and cracked stone stairway brought us up to a solid metal doorway labeled in archaic script *MARK III BEACON – AUTHORIZED PERSONNEL ONLY*. The trusting builders counted on the sign to do the whole job, for there wasn't a trace of a lock on the door. One lizard merely turned the handle and we were inside the beacon.

I unzipped the front of my camouflage suit and pulled out the blueprints. With the faithful priests stumbling after me, I located the control room and turned on the lights. There was a residue of charge in the emergency batteries, just enough to give a dim light. The meters and indicators looked to be in good shape; if anything, unexpectedly bright from constant polishing.

I checked the readings carefully and found just what I had suspected. One of the eager lizards had managed to open a circuit box and had polished the switches inside. While doing this, he had thrown one of the switches and that had caused the trouble.

*R*ather, that had *started* the trouble. It wasn't going to be ended by just reversing the water-valve switch. This valve was supposed to be used only for repairs, after the pile was damped. When the water was cut off with the pile in operation, it had started to overheat and the automatic safeties had dumped the charge down the pit.

I could start the water again easily enough, but there was no fuel left in the reactor.

I wasn't going to play with the fuel problem at all. It would be far easier to install a new power plant. I had one in the ship that was about a tenth the size of the ancient bucket of bolts and produced at least four times the power. Before I sent for it, I checked over the rest of the beacon. In 2000 years, there should be *some* sign of wear.

The old boys had built well, I'll give them credit for that. Ninety percent of the machinery had no moving parts and had suffered no wear whatever. Other parts they had beefed up, figuring they would wear, but slowly. The water-feed pipe from the roof, for example. The pipe walls were at least three meters thick — and the pipe opening itself no bigger than my head. There were some things I could do, though, and I made a list of parts.

The parts, the new power plant and a few other odds and ends were chuted into a neat pile on the ship. I checked all the parts by screen before they were loaded in a metal crate. In the darkest hour before dawn, the heavy-duty eye dropped the crate outside the temple and darted away without being seen.

I watched the priests through the pryeye while they tried to open it. When they had given up, I boomed orders at them through a speaker in the crate. They spent most of the day sweating the heavy box up through the narrow temple stairs and I enjoyed a good sleep. It was resting inside the beacon door when I woke up.

*T*he repairs didn't take long, though there was plenty of groaning from the blind lizards when they heard me ripping the wall open to get at the power leads. I even hooked a gadget to the water pipe so their Holy Waters would have the usual refreshing radioactivity when they started flowing again. The moment this was all finished, I did the job they were waiting for.

I threw the switch that started the water flowing again.

There were a few minutes while the water began to gurgle down through the dry pipe. Then a roar came from outside the pyramid that must have shaken its stone walls. Shaking my hands once over my head, I went down for the eye-burning ceremony.

The blind lizards were waiting for me by the door and looked even unhappier than usual. When I tried the door, I found out why — it was bolted and barred from the other side.

"It has been decided," a lizard said, "that you shall remain here forever and tend the Holy Waters. We will stay with you and serve your every need."

A delightful prospect, eternity spent in a locked beacon with three blind lizards. In spite of their hospitality, I couldn't accept.

"What — you dare interfere with the messenger of your ancestors!" I had the speaker on full volume and the vibration almost shook my head off.

The lizards cringed and I set my Solar for a narrow beam and ran it around the door jamb. There was a great crunching and banging from the junk piled against it, and then the door swung free. I threw it open. Before they could protest, I had pushed the priests out through it.

The rest of their clan showed up at the foot of the stairs and made a great ruckus while I finished welding the door shut. Running through the crowd, I faced up to the First Lizard in his tub. He sank slowly beneath the surface.

"What lack of courtesy!" I shouted. He made little bubbles in the water. "The ancestors are annoyed and have decided to forbid entrance to the Inner Temple forever; though, out of kindness, they will let the waters flow. Now I must return — on with the ceremony!"

The torture-master was too frightened to move, so I grabbed out his hot iron. A touch on the side of my face dropped a steel plate over my eyes, under the plastiskin. Then I jammed the iron hard into my phony eye-sockets and the plastic gave off an authentic odor.

A cry went up from the crowd as I dropped the iron and staggered in blind circles. I must admit it went off pretty well.

*B*efore they could get anymore bright ideas, I threw the switch and my plastic pterodactyl sailed in through the door. I couldn't see it, of course, but I knew it had arrived when the grapples in the claws latched onto the steel plates on my shoulders.

I had got turned around after the eye-burning and my flying beast hooked onto me backward. I had meant to sail out bravely, blind eyes facing into the sunset; instead, I faced the crowd as I soared away, so I made the most of a bad situation and threw them a snappy military salute. Then I was out in the fresh air and away.

When I lifted the plate and poked holes in the seared plastic, I could see the pyramid growing smaller behind me, water gushing out of the base and a happy crowd of reptiles sporting in its radioactive rush. I counted off on my talons to see if I had forgotten anything.

One: The beacon was repaired.

Two: The door was sealed, so there should be no more sabotage, accidental or deliberate.

Three: The priests should be satisfied. The water was running again, my eyes had been duly burned out, and they were back in business. Which added up to —

Four: The fact that they would probably let another repairman in, under the same conditions, if the beacon conked out again. At least I had done nothing, like butchering a few of them, that would make them antagonistic toward future ancestral messengers.

I stripped off my tattered lizard suit back in the ship, very glad that it would be some other repairman who'd get the job.

HARRY HARRISON

www.ingramcontent.com/pod-product-compliance
Lightning Source LLC
Chambersburg PA
CBHW031906170626
46807CB00004B/1920